EASY LETTER NOTES

LETTER-ONLY PIANO PLAYING

Christmas Carols & Songs

Book design 1st edition 2023

Play In One Day - playinoneday.com
Publisher

contact@playinoneday.com
Contact email

CONTENTS

Basics of learning to play the piano

Sound names:

Each key on the keyboard (or any other keyboard instrument) corresponds to one of the letters:
C, D, E, F, G, A, B. You can best understand this by looking at the picture below.

Some of the white keys have shorter black keys in between.

The black key to the right of the C key is the C# key.
The black key to the right of the D key is the D# key.
There is no black key to the right of the E key.
The black key to the right of the F key is the F# key.
The black key to the right of the G key is the G# key.
The black key to the right of the A key is the A# key.

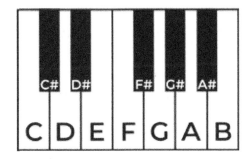

Description of the entire keyboard:

The above pattern (C, D, E, F, G, A, B) is repeated several times on your instrument's keyboard. In order not to confuse the letters, we add numbers to them depending on their position on the keyboard.

In the very centre of the keyboard, the letters have no numbers added.
They are numbered 2 to the right of the keyboard, and 3 further to the right.
They are numbered -2 to the left of the keyboard, and -3 further to the left.

as in the drawing. *If you have a keyboard with less keys, find the centre C sound and disregard the lowest and the highest sounds.*

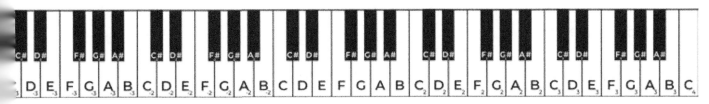

Learning to play in three steps

STEP 1 - Practice the key names and play with your right hand.

If you are just starting to learn to play the piano, a good way to remember all the names of the keys (C, D, E, F, G, A, B) is to only learn to play with your right hand.

Just ignore the left hand notes (the ones in the squares) and play only with your right hand. Thanks to this, you will practice the names of the keys well and get used to the keyboard.

You will switch to the two-handed play once you have mastered the names of all the keys.

Always listen to the recordings (page 13) before learning to play!

STEP 2 - Add your left hand to the right one.

Do you already know key names? Can you already play with your right hand?
If yes, add your left hand.

Now if you see a square with a letter in the middle above the note for your right hand - press this key with your left hand.

Continue the play with your right hand and keep the key pressed with your left hand for some time, but no longer than when you come across the next square with the letter in the middle.

STEP 3 - A two-handed play with chords.

Two-handed play is no longer a problem for you?

Instead of playing only single notes with your left hand, play whole chords (3 keys at the same time).

If, for example, you see the letter "C" in a square, then instead of playing only the C note with your left hand, play the entire C chord.

You will find a list of all the chords and keys you need to press to play them in the attached chord table (page 10).

It is best to practice all the chords in the song first before playing it.

Frequently asked questions

1. What do our letter notes look like:

Our letter notes allow you to play with two hands. Larger letters represent the notes for the right hand. Smaller letters in the squares represent the notes (chords) for the left hand.

2. Where to play the chords:

If you're wondering where to play the chords, look at the figure below:

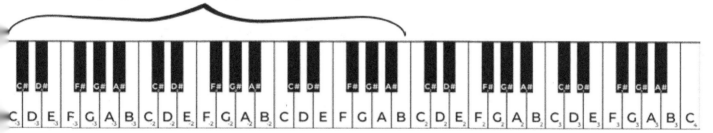

In fact, you can also play the chords where you think they sound good. It's not specifically defined.

3. There is only a verse and a chorus in the notes, how do you play the whole song?

In the notes, you will most often find a verse and a chorus. The songs are arranged as follows:

verse - chorus - verse - chorus - verse - chorus etc.

Therefore, to play the whole thing - just repeat the verse and chorus (each verse and each chorus is played to the same melody).

Sometimes there is only a chorus in the notes. This means the song has no verse and the layout is:

chorus - chorus - chorus etc.

That's all you need to know
to play the letter notes.

Major chords

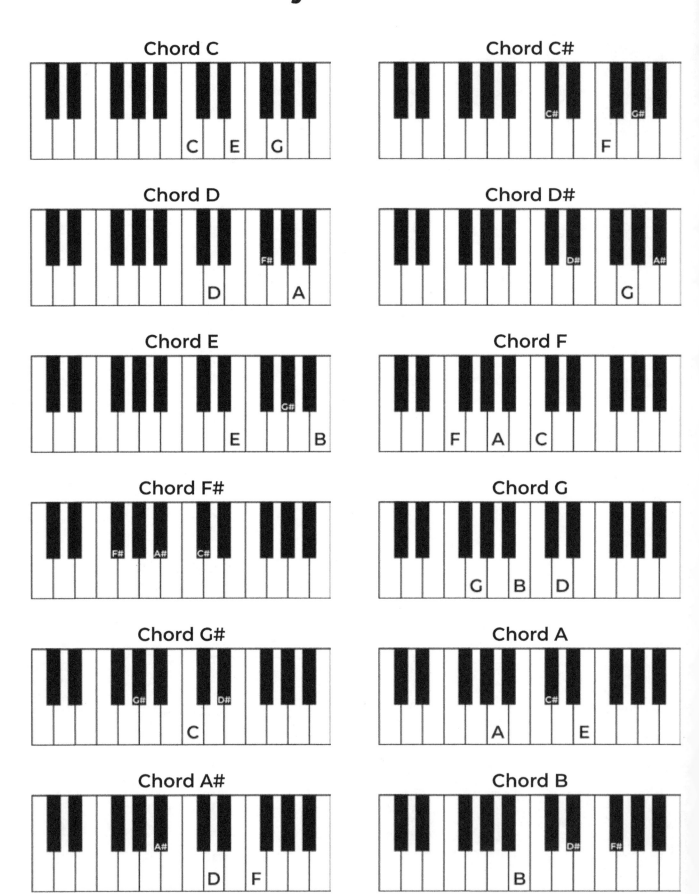

Minor chords

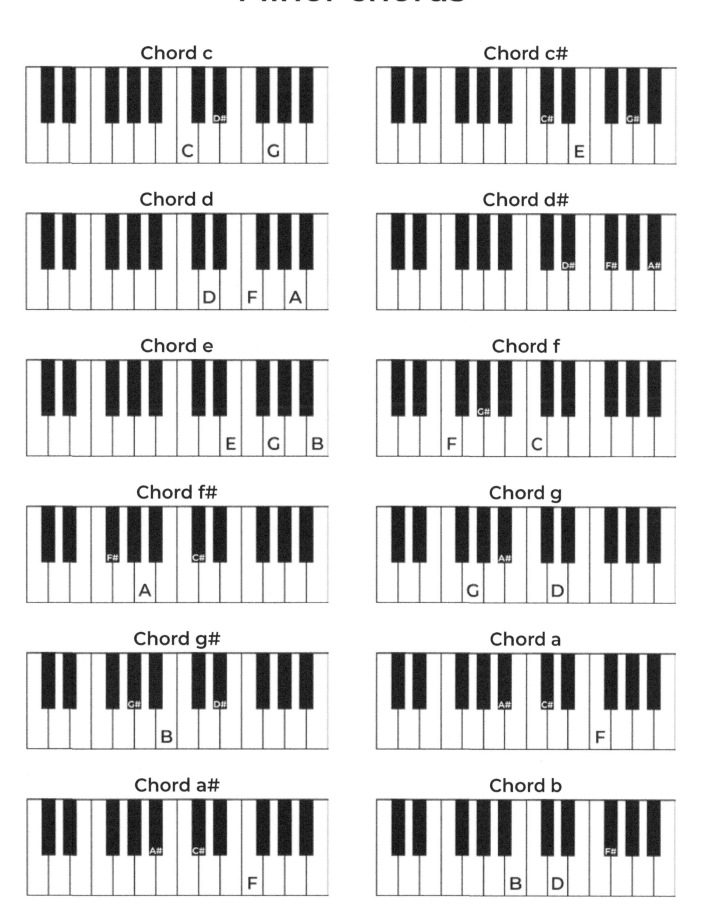

Videos to all of the songs can be found there:

playinoneday.com/ELNcarols

Cut-outs for your piano

CUT THERE CUT THERE CUT THERE CUT THERE CUT THERE CUT THERE

C_{-3} D_{-3} E_{-3} F_{-3} G_{-3} A_{-3} B_{-3}

C_{-2} D_{-2} E_{-2} F_{-2} G_{-2} A_{-2} B_{-2}

C D E F G A B

C_2 D_2 E_2 F_2 G_2 A_2 B_2

C_3 D_3 E_3 F_3 G_3 A_3 B_3

$A_{-3}\#$ $A_{-2}\#$ $A\#$ $A_2\#$ $A_3\#$
$G_{-3}\#$ $G_{-2}\#$ $G\#$ $G_2\#$ $G_3\#$
$F_{-3}\#$ $F_{-2}\#$ $F\#$ $F_2\#$ $F_3\#$
$D_{-3}\#$ $D_{-2}\#$ $D\#$ $D_2\#$ $D_3\#$
$C_{-3}\#$ $C_{-2}\#$ $C\#$ $C_2\#$ $C_3\#$

How to set up cut-outs

Place the cut-outs on your keyboard as shown in the diagram on page 5.

If your instrument has more keys than in the diagram, start labeling your keyboard from the central C sound. Go left and right until you run out of our cut-outs. (But don't worry you won't need remaining keys).

If you would like to print out cut-outs (with letters) individually, you may find the file here:
playinoneday.com/ELNstickers
(it may be useful if you want to print it on self-adhesive paper or if you need another set of them)

Level 1

VIDEO: playinoneday.com/ELNcarols/#19

Christ Was Born On Christmas Day

C E F [C] G C E F [C] G

When Christ was born on Christmas Day,

C E F [C] G E C E [G] D

When Christ was born on Christmas Day,

E E D [C] C C E G G [F] G F

Oh how I want to be in that number,

F E F [C] G E [F] C D [C] C

When Christ was born on Christmas Day.

Twelve Days of Christmas

G_{-2} G_{-2} [C] G_{-2} C C [C] C B_{-2}

On the first day of Christmas,

C D [G] E F D [C] E

my true love gave to me:

[G] G A F E C D B_{-2} [C] C

A partridge in a pear tree.

G_{-2} G_{-2} [C] G_{-2} G_{-2} C C [C] C B_{-2}

On the second day of Christmas,

C D [G] E F D [C] E

my true love gave to me:

[G] G D E F

Two turtle doves,

E F [G] G A F E C D B_{-2} [C] C

And a partridge in a pear tree.

Difficulty
★☆☆

Jolly Old Saint Nicholas

[C] E E E E [G] D D D

Jolly old St. Nicholas

[a] C C C C [e] E

Lean your ear this way

[F] A₋₂ A₋₂ A₋₂ A₋₂ G₋₂ G₋₂ [C] C

Don't you tell a single soul

[G] B₋₂ C D E D

What I'm going to say

[C] E E E E [G] D D D

Christmas Eve is coming soon

[a] C C C C [e] E

Now, you dear old man

[F] A₋₂ A₋₂ A₋₂ A₋₂ G₋₂ G₋₂ [C] C

Whisper what you'll bring to me

[G] D C D E [C] C

Tell me if you can.

21

O Christmas Tree

G₋₂ [C] C C C [G] D [C] E E

O Christmas Tree, O Christmas Tree

E D E F [G] B₋₂ [C] D C

How lovely are your branches!

G₋₂ [C] C C C [G] D [C] E E

O Christmas Tree, O Christmas Tree

E D E F [G] B₋₂ [C] D C

How lovely are your branches!

G [C] G E A G [d] G F F

Your boughs so green in summertime,

F [G] F D G F [C] F E E

Stay bravely green in wintertime.

G₋₂ [C] C C C [G] D [a] E E

O Christmas Tree, O Christmas Tree

E D E F [G] B₋₂ [C] D C

How lovely are your branches!

VIDEO: playinoneday.com/ELNcarols/#23

O Little Town of Bethlehem

G₋₂ [C]C C C D [C]E D E F G

O little town of Bethlehem,

E [G]F E C D D [C]C

how still we see thee lie.

G₋₂ [C]C C C D [C]E D E F G

Above thy deep and dreamless sleep

E [G]F E C D D [C]C

The silent stars go by;

C [e]E G A [G]G F E D [C]C D E F G

Yet in thy dark streets shineth

G₋₂ [a]C E [d]D C [G]G₋₂

The everlasting light

G₋₂ [C]C C C D [C]E D E F G

The hopes and fears of all the years

E [G]F E C D D [C]C

Are met in thee tonight.

Difficulty
★☆☆

I Saw Three Ships

G C₂ C₂ D₂ E₂ G₂ E₂ D₂

I saw three ships come sailing in,

F₂ E₂ C₂ C₂ E₂ D₂ B G

On Christmas Day, on Christmas Day,

G C₂ C₂ D₂ E₂ G₂ E₂ D₂

I saw three ships come sailing in,

F₂ E₂ C₂ C₂ D₂ E₂ D₂ C₂

On Christmas Day in the morning.

VIDEO: playinoneday.com/ELNcarols/#25

In the Bleak Midwinter

[C] E F G E [a] D C

In the bleak midwinter

[F] D E D A₋₂ [d] D

Frosty wind made moan,

[C] E F G E [a] D C

Earth stood hard as iron,

[F] D E D [G] C [C] C

Water like a stone.

[F] F E F G [F] A E

Snow had fallen, snow on snow,

[C] G E D C [G] B₋₂

Snow on snow.

[C] E F G E [a] D C

In the bleak midwinter.

[F] D E D [G] C [C] C

Long ago.

25

Once in Royal David's City

G₋₂ B₋₂ [C] C C C B₋₂ C D [C] D C

Once in royal David's city

C E [a] G E E D C B₋₂ [C] C

Stood a lowly cattle shed,

G₋₂ B₋₂ [C] C C C B₋₂ C D [C] D C

Where a mother layed her baby

C E [a] G E E D C B₋₂ [C] C

in a manger for his bed:

A A [C] G C [G] F F [C] E

Mary was that mother mild,

A A [C] G E E D C B₋₂ [C] C

Jesus Christ her little child.

VIDEO: playinoneday.com/ELNcarols/#27

Pat-a-Pan

A A E₂[a] E₂ D₂ E₂ C₂[a]

Willie, bring your little drum;

B C₂ D₂ B₂ E₂[a] C₂ B[E]

Robin, bring your flute and come,

B C₂ B[E] G# A B C₂[a]

We'll be joyous as you play,

A B C₂ D₂ E₂[a]

Toora-loora-loo,

D₂ E₂ D₂ C₂ B[E]

Pat-a-pat-a-pan,

B C₂ B[E] G# A B C₂[a]

We'll be joyous as you play,

B C₂ D₂[a] B E₂[E] C₂[a] A[E]

On a Merry Christmas Day!

27

The Holly and the Ivy

C C C C A G E

The holy and the ivy

C C C C A G

When they are both full grown

G F E D C E E A₋₂ A₋₂ G₋₂

Of all trees that are in the wood,

C D E F E D C

The holy bears the crown.

C C C C C A G E

On the rising of the sun

C C C C C A G

And the running of the deer

G F E D C E A₋₂ A₋₂ G₋₂ C

The playing of the merry organ,

D E F E D C

Sweet singing in the choir.

VIDEO: playinoneday.com/ELNcarols/#29

The First Noel

E D C̄ D E F Ḡ A B C̄₂ B A Ḡ

The First Noel the angel did say

A B C̄₂ B A Ḡ A B C̄₂ Ḡ F Ē

Was to certain poor shepherds, in fields as they lay;

E D C̄ D E F Ḡ A B C̄₂ B A Ḡ

In fields where they lay, keeping their sheep,

A B C̄₂ B A Ḡ A B C̄₂ Ḡ F Ē

On a cold winter's night that was so deep.

E D C̄ D E F Ḡ C̄₂ B A A B Ḡ

Noel, Noel, Noel, Noel,

C̄₂ B A Ḡ A B C̄₂ Ḡ F Ē

Born is the King of Israel!

Lo, How a Rose E'er Blooming

G G G A G G E
[C] [G]

Lo, how a Rose e'er blooming

F E D C B₋₂ C
[d]   [a]   [C]

From tender stem hath sprung!

G G G A G G E
[C] [G]

Of Jesse's lineage coming,

F E D C B₋₂ C
[d]   [a]   [C]

As men of old have sung.

E D B₋₂ C A₋₂ G₋₂ B₋₂
[d]   [G]

It came, a flow'ret bright,

G G G A G G E
[C] [G]

Amid the cold of winter,

F E D C B₋₂ C
[d]   [a]   [C]

When half spent was the night.

VIDEO: playinoneday.com/ELNcarols/#31

What Child Is This?

D F G A B A G E C D

What child is this who, laid to rest

E F D D C D E C# A₋₂

On Mary's lap is sleeping?

D F G A B A G E C D

Whom angels greet with anthems sweet,

E F E D C# B₋₂ C# D D

While shepherds watch are keeping?

C₂ C₂ B A G E C D

This, this is Christ the King,

E F D D C D E C# A₋₂

Whom shepherds guard and angels sing;

C₂ C₂ B A G E C D

Haste, haste to bring Him laud,

E F E D C# B₋₂ C# D D

The Babe, the Son of Mary.

Level 2

★★☆

VIDEO: playinoneday.com/ELNcarols/#35

He Has a Red, Red Coat

G A G $\boxed{\text{C}}$C$_2$ C$_2$ G

He has a red, red coat

A G $\boxed{\text{C}}$C$_2$ C$_2$ G

And a red, red hat

G $\boxed{\text{C}}$C$_2$ C$_2$ G

His boots are black

A G $\boxed{\text{C}}$C$_2$ C$_2$ C$_2$ G

And he carries a sack.

G G A $\boxed{\text{G}}$B B B B D$_2$

He has a twinkle in his eye

G A $\boxed{\text{G}}$B B D$_2$

And a friendly smile,

G G $\boxed{\text{G}}$G G E$_2$ C$_2$ D$_2$ $\boxed{\text{C}}$C$_2$

And his name is Santa Claus.

Come, Thou Long-Expected Jesus

Difficult ★★☆

[C] C D C D E [F] F E D C D

Come, Thou long expected Jesus

[C] G F E E [d] D C D [C] C

Born to set Thy people free;

[C] C D C D E [F] F E D C D

From our fears and sins release us,

[C] G F E E [d] D C D [C] C

Let us find our rest in Thee.

[e] G G G F E [d] F F F E D

Israel's strength and consolation,

[C] E E E E F G [d] G F E D

Hope of all the earth Thou art;

[C] G E G F D F [C] E C E D F D

Dear desire of every nation,

[C] G G A G F E D [G] [C] C

Joy of every longing heart.

VIDEO: playinoneday.com/ELNcarols/#37

Up On the Housetop

[C] G G A G E D [C] C E G

Up on the housetop reindeer pause,

[F] A A G E D [C] G [G] G

Out jumps good old Santa Claus

[C] G G A G E D [C] C E G

Down thru the chimney with lots of toys

[F] A A A [C] G G E D [G] G [C] C

All for the little ones, Christmas joys

F F A [F] G G G E [C]

Ho ho ho, who wouldn't go?

[G] D D F [C] E G G C E

Ho ho ho, who wouldn't go-o?

[C] G G A G E F [F] G A

Up on the housetop, click, click, click

[C] G G A G G E D [G] G [C] C

Down thru the chimney with good Saint Nick.

37

O Come, Emmanuel

A₋₂ C[a] E E[d] E D F[G] E D C[C]

Oh come, oh come, Emmanuel,

D E[C] C A₋₂ C[F] D B₋₂ A_{-2[G]} G_{-2[e]} A_{-2[a]}

And ransom captive Israel,

D D[d] A₋₂ A₋₂ B₋₂ C[a] B_{-2[D]} A₋₂ G_{-2[G]}

That mourns in lonely exile here,

C D[G] E E[e] E D[d] F E D C[C]

Until the Son of God appear.

G G[G] E[a] E[e] E D[C] F[d] E D C[G] [C]

Rejoice! Rejoice! Emmanuel

D[G] E[C] C A_{-2[F]} C D B_{-2[d]} A₋₂ G_{-2[e]} A_{-2[a]}

Shall come to you, o Israel!

VIDEO: playinoneday.com/ELNcarols/#39

We Three Kings

[a] [a] [E] [a]
E D C A₋₂ B₋₂ C B₋₂ A₋₂

We three kings of orient are

[a] [a] [E] [a]
E D C A₋₂ B₋₂ C B₋₂ A₋₂

Bearing gifts we traverse afar

[C] [G] [C] [C]
C C D D E E G F

Field and fountain, moor and mountain,

[d] [E] [a]
E D E D C B₋₂ A₋₂

Following yonder star.

[G] [C] [C] [C] [F] [C]
B₋₂ D C C C G₋₂ C A₋₂ C

O star of wonder, star of night

[C] [C] [C] [F] [C]
C C C G₋₂ C A₋₂ C

Star with royal beauty bright,

[a] [G] [d] [G]
C C D E F E D E

Westward leading, still proceeding,

[a] [a] [F] [C]
C C C A₋₂ C A₋₂ C

Guide with thy perfect light.

39

Difficulty
★★☆

Coventry Carol

[a] [a] [G] [E]
A A G# A C₂ B B B A G#

Lully, lulla, Thou little tiny Child

[a] [d] [a]
A B C₂ D₂ B A

Bye, bye, lully, lullay

[a] [G] [a] [a]
E₂ D₂ D₂ B B A A

A little tiny Child,

[d] [A]
A G# A D₂ B C#₂

Bye, bye, lully, lullay

[a] [a] [G] [E]
A A G# A C₂ B A G#

O sisters too, how may we do

[a] [d] [a]
A B C₂ D₂ B A

For to preserve this day, this

[d] [G] [G] [E]
E₂ D₂ C₂ B B C₂ B A G#

Poor youngling for whom we do sing,

[a] [d] [E] [a]
A B C₂ D₂ B A

Bye, bye, lully, lullay.

Difficulty ★★☆

O Come, Little Children

G [C]G E G [a]G E

O come, little children,

G [d]F D F [C]E

O come, one and all,

G [C]G E G [a]G E

To Bethlehem's table

G [d]F D F [C]E

in Bethlehem's stall

E [G]D D D [G]F F F

And see with rejoicing this

[C]E E E [F]A

Glorious sight

A [C]G G G [a]C₂ G E

Our father in heaven

[d]F [G]D B₋₂ [C]C

Has sent us this night.

41

Blue Christmas

[C] G$_{-2}$ C D [C] E [C] E D C [G] B$_{-2}$ D

I'll have a blue Christmas without you.

[G] G$_{-2}$ B$_{-2}$ D F [G] F F [G] F E D [C] C E

I'll be so blue just thinking about you.

[C] E F [G] G F E [A] G F E [d] D E F [f] F

Decorations of red on a green Christmas tree

[C] E D C [a] E D C [G] B$_{-2}$ [G] B$_{-2}$ C [D] C# [G] D

Won't be the same dear, if you're not here with me.

G$_{-2}$ C D [C] E [C] E D C [G] B$_{-2}$ D

And when those blue snowflakes start falling

[G] G$_{-2}$ B$_{-2}$ D [G] F [G] F F E D [C] C E

That's when those blue memories start calling

[C] E F [G] G F E [A] G

You'll be doing all right.

F E D E F A

With your Christmas of white

A$_{-2}$ G$_{-2}$ B$_{-2}$ C D E D C

But I'll have a blue, blue, blue, blue Christmas.

Angels From the Realms of Glory

[C] E E E G G F E D

Angels from the realms of glory,

[a] E D E G E D [C] C

Wing your flight all 'round the earth.

[C] E E E G G F E D

Ye who sang creation's story,

[a] E D E G E D [C] C

Now proclaim messiah's birth.

[C] G A G F E F [d] G F E D

Glo-

[C] E F E D C D G G_{-2} G_{-2}

Ooo

[C] C D E F E [F] [G] D [C] C

In excelsis Deo

[C] G A G F E D [G] G G_{-2} G_{-2}

Gloria

C D E F

in excelsis

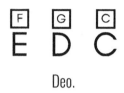

E D C

Deo.

Carol of the Bells

Difficult

C_2 B C_2 A C_2 B C_2 A

C_2 B C_2 A C_2 B C_2 A

[a] C_2 B C_2 A [G] C_2 B C_2 A

[F] C_2 B C_2 A [a] C_2 B C_2 A

[a] C_2 B C_2 A [G] C_2 B C_2 A

[F] C_2 B C_2 A [a] C_2 B C_2 A

[d] C_2 B C_2 A [a] C_2 B C_2 A

[d] C_2 B C_2 A [a] C_2 B C_2 A

[a] E$_2$ D$_2$ E$_2$ C$_2$ [D] E$_2$ D$_2$ E$_2$ C$_2$

[a] E$_2$ D$_2$ E$_2$ C$_2$ [E] E$_2$ D$_2$ E$_2$ C$_2$

[a] A$_2$ A$_2$ A$_2$ G$_2$ F$_2$ [a] E$_2$ E$_2$ E$_2$ D$_2$ C$_2$

[d] D$_2$ D$_2$ D$_2$ E$_2$ D$_2$ [a] C$_2$ B C$_2$ A

[E] E F# G# A B C$_2$ [a] D$_2$ E$_2$ D$_2$ C$_2$

[E] E F# G# A B C$_2$ [a] D$_2$ E$_2$ D$_2$ C$_2$

$\overset{\boxed{a}}{C_2}$ B C_2 A $\overset{\boxed{d}}{C_2}$ B C_2 A

$\overset{\boxed{a}}{C_2}$ B C_2 A C_2 B C_2 A

C_2 B C_2 A C_2 B C_2 A

Difficulty
★★☆

Frosty the Snowman

[C] G E F [C] G C₂ B C₂ [F] D₂ C₂ B A [C] G

Frosty the snowman was a jolly happy soul

B C₂ [F] D₂ C₂ B A A [G] G C₂ [a] E

With a corncob pipe and a button nose

G A [F] G F E [G] D [C] G

And two eyes made out of coal

[C] G E F [C] G C₂ B C₂ [F] D₂ C₂ B A [C] G

Frosty the snowman is a fairy tale, they say

B C₂ [F] D₂ C₂ B A A [C] G C₂ [a] E

He was made of snow but the children know

G A [d] G F E [G] D [C] C

How he came to life one day.

[F] C A A C₂ C₂ [G] B A [C] G

There must have been some magic in

E [d] F A [G] G F [C] E

That Old top hat they found

49

E D D G G B B D₂

For when they placed it on his head

D₂ C₂ B A G F D

He began to dance around

G E F G C₂

O, Frosty the snowman

B C₂ D₂ C₂ B A G

Was alive as he could be

B C₂ D₂ C₂ B A A G C₂ E

And the children say he could laugh and play

G A G F E D C

Just the same as you and me

G G G G G

Thumpety thump thump

G G G G G

Thumpety thump thump

50

[C]　G　G　F　E　D　[G]

Look at Frosty go

[G]　G　G　G　G　G

Thumpety thump thump

[G]　G　G　G　G　G

Thumpety thump thump

[G]　G　G　G　A　B　[C]　C$_2$

Over the hills of snow.

Ding Dong! Merrily on High

[C] C₂ C₂ D₂ C₂ B A [G] G

Ding dong, merily on high!

G [F] A C₂ C₂ B [C] C₂ C₂

in heav'n the bells are ringing;

[C] C₂ C₂ D₂ C₂ B A [G] G

Ding dong, verily the sky

G [F] A C₂ C₂ B [C] C₂ C₂

is riv'n with angel singing.

[G] G₂ F₂ E₂ F₂ G₂ E₂ [d] F₂ E₂ D₂ E₂ F₂ D₂

Glo-

[C] E₂ D₂ C₂ D₂ E₂ C₂ [d] D₂ C₂ B C₂ D₂ B

-

[C] C₂ B A B C₂ A B A [G] G

Ria,

G [F] A C₂ C₂ B [G] [C] C₂ C₂

Ho-sanna in excelsis!

52

It Came Upon A Midnight Clear

G E₂ B D₂ C₂ A G A

It came upon the midnight clear,

G A B C₂ C₂ D₂ E₂ D₂

That Glorious song of old.

G E₂ B D₂ C₂ A G A G

From angels bending near the earth,

G A A B A G A

To touch their harps of gold.

E₂ E₂ E E F# G# A B C₂

Peace of the earth good will to men

E₂ D₂ C₂ B A B A G

From heavens all gracious king.

G E₂ B D₂ C₂ A G A G

The word in solemn stillness lay,

G A A B A G A

To hear the angels sing.

53

VIDEO: playinoneday.com/ELNcarols/#54

Difficult
★★☆

We Wish You a Merry Christmas

G C₂[C] C₂ D₂ C₂ B A[F] A

We wish you a merry Christmas

A D₂[D] D₂ E₂ D₂ C₂ B[G] G

We wish you a merry Christmas

G E₂[E] E₂ F₂ E₂ D₂ C₂[a] A

We wish you a merry Christmas

G G A[C] D₂[F] B[G] C₂[C]

and a happy new year!

G C₂[C] C₂ D₂ C₂ B A[F] A

We wish you a merry Christmas

A D₂[D] D₂ E₂ D₂ C₂ B[G] G

We wish you a merry Christmas

G E₂[E] E₂ F₂ E₂ D₂ C₂[a] A

We wish you a merry Christmas

G G A[C] D₂[F] B[G] C₂[C]

and a happy new year!

54

G C̲₂ C̲₂ C̲₂ B B C̲₂ B A G

Good tidings we bring to you and your kin

D₂ E̲₂ D₂ D₂ C₂ C₂ G̲₂ G

We wish you a merry Christmas

G G A̲ D₂ B̲ C̲₂

And a happy new year

G C̲₂ C₂ D₂ C₂ B A̲ A

Oh, bring us some figgy pudding

A D̲₂ D₂ E₂ D₂ C₂ B̲ G

Oh, bring us some figgy pudding

G E̲₂ E₂ F₂ E₂ D₂ C̲₂ A

Oh, bring us some figgy pudding

G̲ A̲ D₂ B̲ C̲₂

And bring it right here.

Rudolph, the Red-Nosed Reindeer

A B [F]C$_2$ A F [e]B G E [d]A F D [C]A G

You know Dasher, and Dancer, and Prancer, and Vixen,

[F]C$_2$ A F [e]B G E [d]A F D [C]A G

Comet, and Cupid, and Donne,r and Blitzen,

[a]E E E [F]A

But do you recall

A B [D]C$_2$ C$_2$ C$_2$ B A [G]G

The most famous reindeer of all?

[C]G A G E C$_2$ [C]A G

Rudolph, the red-nosed reindeer

[C]G A G A G C$_2$ [G]B

Had a very shiny nose

[G]F G F D B [G]A G

And if you ever saw it

[G]G A G A G [G]A [C]E

You would even say it glows.

[C] G A G E C$_2$ [C] A G

All of the other reindeer

[C] G A G A G C$_2$ [G] B

Used to laugh and call him names

[G] F G F D B [G] A G

They never let poor Rudolph

[G] G A G A G D$_2$ [C] C$_2$

Join in any reindeer games.

[F] A A C$_2$ A [C] G E G

Then one foggy Christmas Eve

[F] F A [G] G F [C] E

Santa came to say:

[G] D E G A [G] B B B

„Rudolph with your nose so bright,

[D] C$_2$ C$_2$ B A [G] G F D

Won't you guide my sleigh tonight?"

$\boxed{\text{C}}$ $\qquad$ $\boxed{\text{C}}$

G A G E C$_2$ A G

Then how the reindeer loved him

$\boxed{\text{C}}$ $\qquad$ $\boxed{\text{G}}$

G A G A G C$_2$ B

As they shouted out with glee,

$\boxed{\text{G}}$ $\qquad$ $\boxed{\text{G}}$

F G F D B A G

Rudolph the red-nosed reindeer.

$\boxed{\text{G}}$ $\qquad$ $\boxed{\text{C}}$

G A G A G D$_2$ C$_2$

You'll go down in history!

$\boxed{\text{G}}$ $\qquad$ $\boxed{\text{C}}$

G A G A G D$_2$ C$_2$

You'll go down in history!

Difficulty
★★☆

Hark! The Herald Angels Sing

[C]
G C$_2$ C$_2$ B C$_2$ E$_2$ E$_2$ D$_2$
[C] [C] [G]

Hark! The herald angels sing,

[C] [F] [G] [C]
G$_2$ G$_2$ G$_2$ F$_2$ E$_2$ D$_2$ C$_2$

Glory to the new-born king,

[C] [C] [G]
G C$_2$ C$_2$ B C$_2$ E$_2$ E$_2$ D$_2$

Peace on earth, and mercy mild,

[G] [D] [G]
G$_2$ D$_2$ D$_2$ C$_2$ B A G

God and sinners reconciled

[G] [a] [d] [G]
G$_2$ G$_2$ G$_2$ C$_2$ F$_2$ E$_2$ E$_2$ D$_2$

Joyful all ye nations rise

[G] [C] [d] [G]
G$_2$ G$_2$ G$_2$ C$_2$ F$_2$ E$_2$ D$_2$

join the triumph of the skies

[F] [g] [A] [d]
A$_2$ A$_2$ A$_2$ G$_2$ F$_2$ E$_2$ F$_2$

With the angelic host proclaim

[G] [C] [G] [C]
D$_2$ E$_2$ F$_2$ G$_2$ C$_2$ C$_2$ D$_2$ E$_2$

Christ is born in Bethlehem'

59

[F] [g] [A] [d]
A_2 A_2 A_2 G_2 F_2 E_2 F_2

Hark! The herald angels sing,

[G] [C] [G] [C]
D_2 E_2 F_2 G_2 C_2 C_2 D_2 C_2

Glory to the new-born king.

Let It Snow!

difficulty ★★☆

G₋₂ G₋₂ [C] G G F E D [G] C [C] G₋₂

Oh, the weather outside is frightful

G₋₂ G₋₂ D C [e] D C D C [D] B₋₂ [G] G₋₂

But the fire is so delightful

A₋₂ [d] A A G [A] F E [d] D

Since we've no place to go

B A [G] G G F E E D [C] C

Let it snow! Let it snow! Let it snow!

G₋₂ [C] G G F E [G] D C [C] G₋₂

It doesn't show signs of stopping

G₋₂ G₋₂ D C [e] D C D C [D] B₋₂ [G] G₋₂

And I brought some corn for popping

A₋₂ [d] A A G [A] F E [d] D

The lights are turned down low

B A [G] G G F E E D [C] C

Let it snow! Let it snow! Let it snow!

B₋₂ C D̲[G] E D B₋₂̲[a] G D̲[b] ̲[e]

When we finally kiss goodnight

B₋₂ D C̲[a] C B₋₂ A₋₂̲[D] G₋₂ A₋₂ B₋₂̲[G]

How I'll hate going out in the storm

B₋₂ C D̲[G] E D B₋₂̲[a] G D̲[b] ̲[E]

But if you'll really hold me tight

G̲[A] F# G F# ̲[D] E D G̲[G]

All the way home I'll be warm

G₋₂ G̲[C] G F E D C̲[C] G₋₂

The fire is slowly dying

G₋₂ G₋₂ D̲[e] C D̲[D] C B₋₂̲[G] G₋₂

And, my dear, we're still goodbyin'

A₋₂ A̲[d] A G F̲[A] E D̲[d]

As long as you love me so

B A G̲[G] G F E E D C̲[C]

Let it snow! Let it snow! Let it snow!

Difficulty
★★☆

Winter Wonderland

Sleigh bells ring, are you listening?

In the lane, snow is glistening

A beautiful sight

We're happy tonight

Walking in a winter wonderland

Gone away is the bluebird

Here to stay is a new bird

To sing a love song

[G] A G G G F

While we stroll along

[D] E E E [G] D D D [C] C

Walking in a winter wonderland

[E] B$_{-2}$ B$_{-2}$ G# G# [A] C# C# A A [E] G# E

In the meadow, we can build a snowman

[E] B$_{-2}$ B$_{-2}$ G# G# [A] C# C# A A [E] G#

We'll pretend that he is Parson Brown

[G] D D B B [C] E E

He'll say, are you married?

C$_2$ C$_2$ [G] B G

We'll say, no man

G [e] B B E E [D] A A D D [G] G

But you can do the job when you're in town

G G G [C] G G E [e] G [A]

Later on, we'll conspire

64

G G G[d] G G F G[d]

As we dream by the fire

G B[G] B B A

To face unafraid

A G[G] G G F

The plans that we've made

E[D] E E E D D D D C[C]

Walking in a winter wonderland.

Here We Come a Caroling

[C] C D E D C D E

Here we come a-caroling

D [C] C G G G G G

Among the leaves so green.

[a] A [C] A G E [e] G [a] F E

Here we come a-wandering so

[G] D C D E F

Fair to be seen.

E F [C] G C₂ A G

Love and joy come to you,

E F [C] G G C₂ A G

And to you your wassail, too,

E F [C] G A E [G] F D C B₋₂

And God bless you and send you a

[C] C D E C [F] F

Happy New Year!

C   G   C

E F G A E F D C B₋₂ C

And God send you a Happy New Year!

Difficult
★★☆

Have Yourself a Merry Little Christmas

[C] C E [a] G [d] C₂ G F E D [G] C D

Have yourself a merry little Christmas

[C] C E G [a] C₂ G [d] [G]

Let your heart be light

[C] E G [a] C₂

From now on

E₂ [d] D₂ C₂ B A [G] G F [E] E [A] [d] [G]

Our troubles will be out of sight

[C] C E [a] G C₂ [d] G F E D [G] C D

Have yourself a merry little Christmas

[C] C E G [a] C₂ G [d] [G]

Make the yuletide gay

[C] E G [a] C₂

From now on

E₂ D₂ C₂ B A [E] G G# B [a] C₂ [g] [C]

Our troubles will be miles away

[F] E₂ [f] E₂ E₂ D₂ C₂ B [C] C₂ D₂

Here we are as in olden days

C₂ B [d] A B C₂ [G] B [e] B

Happy golden days of yore

[a] C₂ C₂ [B] C₂ B A G [e] A B

Faithful friends who are dear to us

[G] G A B [G] C₂ D₂ [D] D [G] G

Gather near to us once more

[C] C E G [a] C₂ [d] G F E D [G] C D

Through the years we all will be together

[C] C E G [a] C₂ [d] G [G]

If the fates allow

[C] E G [a] C₂ E₂ F₂ E₂ D₂ C₂ B [E] D₂ [a] E₂ [g]

Hang a shining star upon the highest bough

[C] E₂ [F] E₂ F A C₂ [d] E₂ D₂ C₂ B [G] A B [C] C₂

And have yourself a merry little Christmas now.

Level 3

★★★

VIDEO: playinoneday.com/ELNcarols/#71

When the Saints Go Marching In

C_2 E_2 F_2 $\boxed{C}$ G_2 C_2 E_2 F_2 $\boxed{C}$ G_2

When the saints go marching in,

C_2 E_2 F_2 $\boxed{C}$ G_2 E_2 C_2 E_2 $\boxed{G}$ D_2

When the saints go marching in,

E_2 E_2 D_2 $\boxed{C}$ C_2 C_2 $\boxed{C}$ E_2 G_2 G_2 $\boxed{F}$ G_2 F_2

Lord, how I want be in that number,

E_2 F_2 $\boxed{C}$ G_2 E_2 C_2 $\boxed{G}$ D_2 $\boxed{C}$ C_2

When the saints go marching in.

Santa Baby

G [C] C₂ A [a] C₂ D₂ [D] D#₂ E₂ D#₂ E₂

$$G \quad \boxed{C}\,C_2 \quad A \quad \boxed{a}\,C_2 \quad D_2 \quad \boxed{D}\,D\#_2 \quad E_2 \quad D\#_2 \quad E_2$$

Santa baby, just slip a Sable

$$\boxed{G}\,D_2 \quad C_2 \quad A \quad G \quad \boxed{C}\,C_2 \quad A \quad \boxed{a}$$

Under the tree for me

$$\boxed{D}\,D\#_2 \quad E_2 \quad \boxed{G}\,D_2 \quad C_2 \quad A \quad G \quad \boxed{C}$$

Been an awful good girl

$$G \quad \boxed{C}\,C_2 \quad A \quad \boxed{a}\,C_2 \quad E_2 \quad \boxed{d}\,G_2 \quad G_2 \quad F_2$$

Santa baby, so hurry down

$$F_2 \quad \boxed{G}\,E_2 \quad G \quad A \quad C_2 \quad \boxed{C}\quad \boxed{d}\quad \boxed{G}$$

The chimney tonight.

Difficulty
★★★

Gloucestershire Wassail

G₋₂ C̄ C C C D E F̄ E D Ḡ G

Waswail, wassail all over the town.

G F̄ D D

Our toast it is

D̄ E F Ē D C D E D̄

White and our ale it is

F Ē D C D E F Ḡ

Our bowl it is made

G F Ē C E D̄

Of the white maple tree,

C D Ē D E F̄

With the wassailing bowl,

E D̄ C B C̄

We'll drink to thee.

The Friendly Beasts

[C] C C D E E [G] D E D [C] C

Jesus our brother kind and good.

F G G [F] A G G D F [C] E

Was humbly born in a stable rude.

C D E E [F] F F E [G] D D [C] E

As the friendly beasts around him stood,

[C] G G F E C [a] D [d] B [G] [C] C
-2

Jesus our brother kind and good.

74

VIDEO: playinoneday.com/ELNcarols/#75

While Shepherds Watched

C E̞ E D C F̞ F E

While shepherds watched their flock by night,

D E̞ G G F# G̞

All seated on the ground.

E A̞ G F E D̞ C B$_{-2}$

The Angel of the lord came down

E D̞ C C̞ B$_{-2}$ C̞

And glory shone around.

Good Christian Men, Rejoice

C C C E F G A G

Good Cristian men, rejoice.

G C C E F G A G

With heart and soul and voice.

G A G F E D C C

Give ye heed to what we say; News! News!

D D E D C D E

Jesus Christ is born today!

G A G F E D C

Ox and ass before Him bow,

C D D E D C D E

and He is in the manger now;

A₋₂ A₋₂ B₋₂ B₋₂ C G

Christ is born today!

E E D D C

Christ is born today!

Christmas is Coming

[C] C C D E C C [C] E D E F [G] G

Christmas is coming, the goose is getting fat,

[C] C_2 B_2 A G [G] A G F [C] E [G] D [C] C

Please put the penny in the old man's hat.

G G [C] E G G G E G

if you haven't got a penny,

G E [C] C_2 B A G A

A ha'penny will do.

B G [C] E G G G E G G G [F] A [G] B [C] C_2

If you haven't got a ha'penny then God bless you!

Jingle Bells

[C] G E₂ D₂ [C] C₂ G
Dashing through the snow,

G G [C] G E₂ D₂ C₂ [F] A
in a one-horse open sleigh

[F] A F₂ E₂ D₂ [G] B
Over the fields we go,

[G] G₂ G₂ F₂ D₂ [C] E₂
Laughing all the way

[C] G E₂ D₂ C₂ [C] G
Bells on bob-tail ring,

[C] G E₂ D₂ C₂ [F] A
Making spirits bright

[F] A F₂ E₂ D₂ [G] G₂ G₂ G₂
What fun it is to ride and sing

[G] G₂ A₂ G₂ F₂ D₂ [C] C₂ G₂
A sleighing song tonight, o!

78

[C] E_2 E_2 E_2 [C] E_2 E_2 E_2

Jingle bells, jingle bells,

[C] E_2 G_2 [F] C_2 D_2 [C] E_2

jingle all the way

[F] F_2 F_2 F_2 F_2 [C] F_2 E_2 E_2 E_2 E_2

O, what fun it is to ride in a

[G] E_2 D_2 D_2 E_2 [G] D_2 G_2

one-horse open sleigh, o!

[C] E_2 E_2 E_2 [C] E_2 E_2 E_2

Jingle bells, jingle bells,

[C] E_2 G_2 [F] C_2 D_2 [C] E_2

jingle all the way

[F] F_2 F_2 F_2 F_2 [C] F_2 E_2 E_2 E_2 E_2

O, what fun it is to ride in a

[G] G_2 G_2 F_2 D_2 [C] C_2

One-horse open sleigh!

O Holy Night

[C]
E E F [C]G

O holy night!

[F]
G A A F A [C]C₂ [C]G

The stars are brightly shining

G E D [C]C E F [G]G F D [C]C

It is the night of our dear Saviour's birth

[C]E E F [C]G G A [F]A F A [C]C₂ [C]G

Long lay the world in sin and error pining

G F# E [e]B G A [B]B C₂ B [e]E

Till He appeared and the soul felt its worth

E [G]G A D [G]G A G [C]C₂ E A [C]G

A thrill of hope the weary world rejoices

G [G]G A D [G]G A G [C]C₂ E [C]G

For yonder breaks a new and glorious morn

[a]C₂ [a]B A [e]B [e]B

Fall on your knees;

80

B D_2 A A A C_2 C_2

Oh, hear the angel voices!

C_2 E_2 D_2 G C_2

O night divine,

B A G G A G G

Oh, the night when Christ was born,

C_2 D_2 G E_2 D_2 C_2

O night divine,

B C_2 D_2 C_2

Oh night, Oh holy night.

Santa Claus is Coming to Town

G E[C] F G G

You better watch out,

G A[F] B C₂ C₂

You better not cry,

G E[C] F G G

You better not pout,

G A[F] G F F

I'm telling you why:

E[C] G C[a] E D[d] F B₋₂[G] C[C]

Santa Claus is coming to town.

G E[C] F G G

He's making a list,

G A[F] B C₂ C₂

He's checking it twice,

G E[C] F G G

He's gonna find out

82

G A G F F
[F above A]

Who's naughty or nice.

E G C E D F B$_{-2}$ C
[C above E, a above G, d above D, G above F, C above B, C above C]

Santa Claus is coming to town.

C$_2$ D$_2$ C$_2$ B C$_2$ A A
[F above D, F above A]

He sees you when you're sleeping,

C$_2$ D$_2$ C$_2$ B C$_2$ A
[F above D, F above A]

And he knows when you're awake,

D$_2$ E$_2$ D$_2$ C#$_2$ D$_2$ B B B
[G above E, G above B]

He knows if you've been bad or good,

B C$_2$ D$_2$ C$_2$ B A G
[D above D, G above G]

So be good for goodness sake.

Difficulty
★★★

I Heard the Bells on Christmas Day

C E D# E E F E F

I heard the bells on christmas day,

F# G C₂ B A A G G

Their old familiar carols play,

G G F E F E D C

And wild and sweet the Words repeat

D E F G A

Of peace of Earth, good

B₋₂ D C

Will to men.

This is the end of the songs...

...but we hope it's not the end of your adventure with the music! **As a little gif**
we've prepared an e-book for you with several additional song. You'll also fin•
songs for other instruments!

Download here: *playinoneday.com/ELNplus*

Love the book? Leave a review!

Help us spread the joy. Your feedback matters and can inspire others to emba•
on this musical journey too. **Share your thoughts on your Amazon account •
via the link below.** Just by clicking "Write a review". Thank you for support!

Leave a review: *playinoneday.com/review3*

Try playing the harmonica

with the series of books
"The easiest Method for playing the harmonica"

There is one instrument that you can play immediately, even after 15 minutes.

To play a song, you just need to blow the air through the numbered holes. This way you play a song!

In our books, you will find hundreds of them.

Thanks to those books, **playing the harmonica is amazingly easy and gives you a lot of fun!**

Scan the QR code
to **Harmonica Tabs** series
and start playing in one day!
playinoneday.com/HT

Try playing the piano

with the series of books
"Numbered Notes"

JUST PRESS THE NUMBERS
AND YOU'LL PLAY THE MELODY!

The theory in those books has been shortened almost to 0.
However, it allows you to play with both hands!

  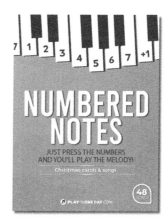

very key has a number assigned to it.In this books, you will find information
on which numbers you should press in order to get a song.
Yes, it is THAT simple :)

Scan the QR code
to **Numbered Notes** series
and start playing in one day!
playinoneday.com/NN

Try playing the piano

with the series of books
"Easy Piano Songs"

From zero to playing the piano beautifully - in 7 days.

The **JOY** of playing your first songs a few moments after receiving this book is indescribable :)

Don't waste countless hours learning tedious rules and traditional notatio symbols. Use our simple notation - and start playing effortlessly!

Learning to play from traditional notes takes time and effort. **Stop tiring yourself out and instead try our specially simplified notes.**

Scan the QR code
to **Easy Piano Songs** series
and start playing!
playinoneday.com/EPS

Try playing the kalimba

with the series of books
"Play The Kalimba In One Day"

Kalimba is easy and intuitive. At the same time,
it makes pleasant, full, and relaxing sounds.

Moreover, it DOES NOT require any previous knowledge or experience.
In order to play a song,
you need to press the numbered keys in the correct order.

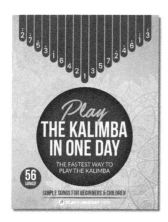 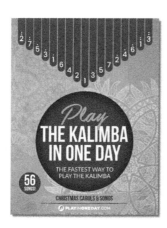 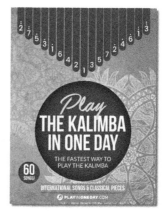

**Thanks to this method starting to play the kalimba is amazingly easy
and gives you great results, i.e. nice play.**

Scan the QR code
to **Kalimba** series
and start playing in one day!
playinoneday.com/K

Try playing the piano

with the series of books
"Easy Letter Notes"

Learn effortlessly with our simple notation
and start making beautiful music with ease!

The perfect notes for beginners.
Specially simplified, with note names and a clear layout

Play the piano without complicated theory
and without difficulty! **No note reading is required!**

Easy Letter Notes make playing the piano
available to everyone regardless of innate talent or age.

Scan the QR code
to **Easy Letter Notes** series
and start playing in one day!
playinoneday.com/ELN

NOTES

NOTES

NOTES

....
....
....
....
....
....
....
....
....
....
....
....
....
....
....
....
....
....
....
....
....
....
....
....
....
....
....

NOTES

NOTES

....
....
....
....
....
....
....
....
....
....
....
....
....
....
....
....
....
....
....
....
....
....
....
....

NOTES

NOTES

NOTES

....
....
....
....
....
....
....
....
....
....
....
....
....
....
....
....
....
....
....
....
....
....
....
....
....
....

Made in the USA
Las Vegas, NV
04 December 2024

13376799R00057